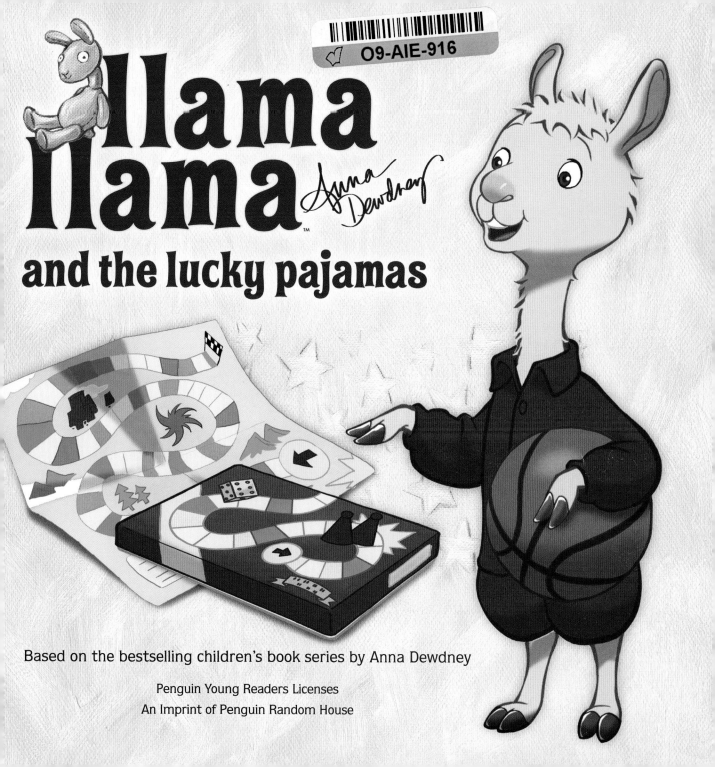

llama llama

Anna Dewdney

and the lucky pajamas

Based on the bestselling children's book series by Anna Dewdney

Penguin Young Readers Licenses

An Imprint of Penguin Random House

O9-AIE-916

PENGUIN YOUNG READERS LICENSES
An Imprint of Penguin Random House LLC

Copyright © Anna E. Dewdney Literary Trust. Copyright © 2018 Genius Brands International, Inc. Published by Penguin Young Readers Licenses, an imprint of Penguin Random House LLC, 345 Hudson Street, New York, New York 10014. Manufactured in China.

ISBN 9781524785017   10 9 8 7 6 5 4 3 2 1

Llama Llama plays in his bedroom one Saturday morning.

He is wearing his red pajamas that Mama Llama just mended for him.

He launches a basketball over his shoulder. It swishes through the hoop.

Llama rushes downstairs. "Mama!" he calls out. "I made the most *amazing* shot with my back turned!"

"Way to go!" says Mama. After they celebrate, Mama asks Llama to make toast for breakfast. Llama is worried that he'll burn the toast like he usually does.

They play Steps and Slides while they wait for the toast to be ready. Llama rolls the dice and cheers, "A six! I win!" He twirls around the kitchen. Suddenly, he stops. "The toast!" he cries.

But the slices pop up perfectly golden brown. Llama grins.

"Things are going *really* well today."

This makes Mama think of something. She digs in the closet and pulls out a goofy hat. Llama laughs.

"This hat brings me luck," Mama tells him.

"What's 'luck'?" asks Llama.

Mama explains that having good luck is when positive things happen to you. She hopes her lucky hat will help her find a parking space at the supermarket.

Llama's eyes light up. "You must have made my pajamas lucky when you mended them, Mama! That's why I had good luck with the basketball, the toast, and the game."

Llama decides to wear his lucky pajamas all day long.

Later, Llama's friends come over to play.

Nelly Gnu grins when Llama answers the door. "Cool outfit, Llama!"

Euclid points out that Llama is wearing pajamas.

Llama says, "Not just any pajamas—my *lucky* pajamas!" To prove how lucky they are, he suggests a game of hide-and-seek. They play, and Llama finds his friends, ***one-two-three.***

"Amazing!" says Euclid. "You found all of us in a superfast flash!"

Euclid wants another test of the lucky pajamas. "What can you try that you've never done before?" he asks Llama.

"I know," says Llama, leading them outside. As they jump rope, Llama exclaims, "We're all jumping exactly together!"

Mama calls from the open window, "I made snacks."

"My favorite apple-honey crisps?" asks Llama.

"Yes," Mama says with surprise.

"How did you know?"

Llama laughs. "My lucky pajamas, of course!"

As they munch in the kitchen, Llama's friends ask if they can borrow his pajamas. They want good luck, too!

Mama Llama interrupts. "I think it's better if everyone sticks with their own clothes."

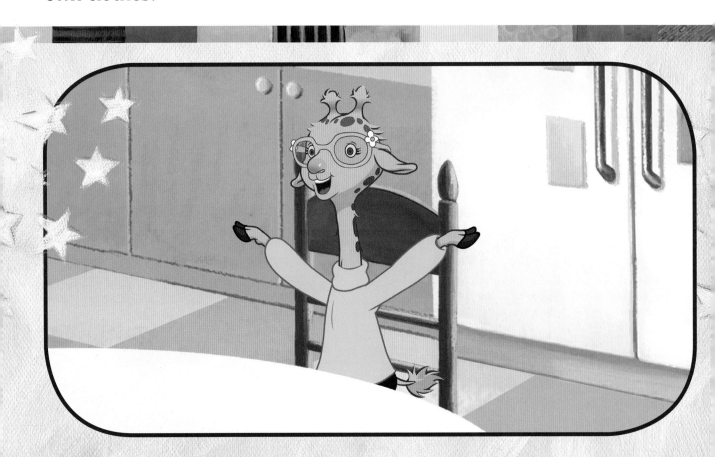

Then Luna has a brilliant idea. She's going to make her own lucky pajamas! Mama Llama has extra cloth, and everyone helps.

But when Luna holds up her new lucky pajamas, they're huge and uneven. Luna cuts them up so everyone can wear a piece.

On Monday, Llama Llama wears his pajamas

underneath his clothes to school.

He finds his friends on the playground. Red pajama pieces are tied to Nelly's forehead, Luna's hair, and Euclid's wrist.

"Yay!" Llama cheers. "We all wore our lucky pajamas!"

Gilroy Goat overhears them talking about how lucky their day will be. He challenges them. "Prove it!" he says.

The friends try jump-roping together. But unlike the day before, their timing is totally off.

Gilroy shakes his head and laughs.

The day only gets worse from there. First, Llama Llama messes up in art class.

At lunch, they frown at servings of soggy, squishy food.

On the playground, none of them are chosen to swing first on the new swings.

"I guess they are **not-so-lucky** red pajamas!" teases Gilroy.

Nelly thinks for a moment and says, "Maybe they're only lucky at your house, Llama."

Everyone rushes to Llama's house after school. Llama does everything he did on Saturday, but nothing turns out right.

The basketball bounces off the rim.

The toast burns to a crisp.

He loses at Steps and Slides.

Llama is close to tears. "Why aren't my lucky pajamas working anymore?"

Mama gives him a hug. "Llama Llama, you actually *are* very lucky,"

she reminds him.

"But nothing went right today," moans Llama.

"That may be," says Mama, "but there's something better and

bigger than luck."

"What's that?" asks Llama.

"Being *fortunate*," replies Mama.

"I am fortunate to have a wonderful home,

kind friends . . . *and* a loving son—**you**!"

Llama Llama smiles brightly. "I'm fortunate to have a mama like you!"

Then he adds, "And great friends, Gram and Grandpa, Fuzzy—

and mended red pajamas."

This gives Llama a great idea. "Let's make an 'I'm Lucky and Fortunate List'!" Everyone takes turns calling out the things they are glad to have. Llama draws pictures.

Books!

Holidays!

Warm wool hats!

Our families!

Hot cocoa with marshmallows!

Our school!

Yummy pancakes!

23

Llama Llama smiles. He is very lucky and fortunate to be making this special list with his wonderful friends.